JUST BE CLAUS

A Christmas Story

By Barbara Joosse • Illustrated by Kim Barnes

PUBLISHED *by* SLEEPING BEAR PRESS™

Once upon a snowstorm,
a jolly little,
round little
baby was born.

"Clausie doesn't look like the other babies in the nursery," said Mom. "And he doesn't even cry!"

"Do you think something's wrong?" asked Dad.

"Psht!" said Grannie. "He's precisely perfect!
He has rosy cheeks and a round little belly
that shakes when he laughs like a bowl full of jelly."

Clausie

By the time Clausie was six,
it was clear he was an unusual child.
He had a surprising laugh.

ho ho ho ha ha ha ha ha

He wore the same red shirt.

Every.

Single.

Day.

No exceptions.

At hockey, Clausie daydreamed.

And sometimes he helped
the other team score
because he didn't want them to feel bad.
Coach Fox was not happy.

Even Clausie's dog was out of the ordinary. Dasher wasn't a regular size.

He was very ...
very ...
BIG.

His super-secret workshop, where he and Granne made things
kazoos, whirligigs, puppets, thingamajigs,

and long leg warmers for Dasher, who was often cold.

But Clausie felt lonely.
His differences made him feel out of place.

One day, Clausie told Grannie his worries. "I'm different!"

"Wonderful!" said Grannie.
"You're one of a kind!"

"But I don't **want** to be different!
I want to be like the other kids."

A tear trickled down Clausie's cheek.
Dasher licked it off.

"You're creative, thoughtful, and generous.
The things that make you different are the best things about you.
Don't try to be like anyone else.
Just be YOU.
Just be Claus."

Clausie was sure Grannie was wrong.

That night, Clausie tossed and turned.
Soon it would be Christmas.
But not even **that** made Clausie feel better.
Dasher rested his head on the comforter
and looked at Clausie with sad eyes.
Then they slept, hand to paw.

That night, the snow came down feathery soft,
then more and more and more
till it seemed like all the world was full to the tippy-top.

By morning, the snowdrifts had shut the roads.
Nothing could get through,
not even the train.

Not even the train?

But the train brought the Christmas packages!

Clausie worried about his neighbors.
They would look under their Christmas trees
and find **nothing** from faraway family. Nothing at all!

No stuffed monkey for Valentina.

No wooden cart for Miguel.

No silver whistle for Coach Fox.

And Fritz, the mailman, wouldn't get his usual pair of leg warmers from great-auntie Mim.

Then Clausie had a brainstorm!
He woke up his family and announced his plan.

Everyone pitched in—wrapping and stacking and filling the sleds.
Then Clausie hooked up Dasher . . .

and delivered presents to his neighbors—
gifts of kazoos, whirligigs, puppets, thingamajigs,
and a very special, very **looong** pair of
leg warmers for Fritz the mailman.

Back home Clausie felt as warm and melty
as a mug of Christmas cocoa.
Grannie was right!
He didn't need to be anybody but himself.
**His differences were the very thing
that helped make others happy.**

And so it was.

That snowy day, Clausie made Christmas special.

It was the first time, but as it turned out . . .

it wasn't the last.

GRANNIE
CLAUS

For Terry & Mary Murphy—neighbors and friends

—Barb

For Sam, who loves Christmas more than anyone I know

xx Kim

SLEEPING BEAR PRESS™

Printed and bound in the United States
10 9 8 7 6 5 4 3 2 1

Library of Congress Cataloging-in-Publication Data
Names: Joosse, Barbara M., author. • Barnes, Kim, illustrator.
Title: Just be Claus : a Christmas story / Barbara Joosse ; and illustrated by Kim Barnes.
Description: Ann Arbor, MI : Sleeping Bear Press, [2021] • Audience: Ages 4-8. Summary: "A little boy named Claus worries that he is different from other kids: he likes to wear red all the time and his favorite hangout is the workshop with his grandmother. His grandmother tells him his differences make him special and a Christmas snowstorm helps Claus appreciate his talents"-- Provided by publisher.
Identifiers: LCCN 2021005328 • ISBN 9781534111011 (hardcover) • Subjects: CYAC: Santa Claus--Fiction. • Christmas--Fiction. • Individuality--Fiction.
Classification: LCC PZ7.J7435 Ju 2021 | DDC [E]--dc23 • LC record available at https://lccn.loc.gov/2021005328